THE HAUNTED BABY

CHOOSE YOUR OWN NIGHTMARE

titles in Large-Print Editions:

CHOOSE YOUR OWN NIGHTMARE #13

THE HAUNTED BABY

by Edward Packard

ILLUSTRATED BY BILL SCHMIDT

Gareth Stevens Publishing
MILWAUKEE

For a free color catalog describing Gareth Stevens' list of high-quality books and multimedia programs, call 1-800-542-2595 (USA) or 1-800-461-9120 (Canada). Gareth Stevens Publishing's Fax: (414) 225-0377. See our catalog, too, on the World Wide Web: http://gsinc.com

Library of Congress Cataloging-in-Publication Data

Packard, Edward, 1931-
    The haunted baby / by Edward Packard ; illustrated by Bill Schmidt.
       p. cm. — (Choose your own nightmare; #13)
       Summary: As babysitter for a two-year-old child, the reader must make choices to determine whether the child is angelic or evil.
      ISBN 0-8368-2070-3 (lib. bdg.)
      1. Plot-your-own stories. [1. Babysitters—Fiction. 2. Horror stories. 3. Plot-your-own stories.] I. Schmidt, Bill, ill. II. Title. III. Series.
PZ7.P1245Hag   1998
[Fic]—dc21   97-39610

This edition first published in 1998 by
Gareth Stevens Publishing
1555 North RiverCenter Drive, Suite 201
Milwaukee, Wisconsin 53212 USA

Printed in the United States of America

1 2 3 4 5 6 7 8 9 02 01 00 99 98

THE HAUNTED BABY

WARNING!

You have probably read books where scary things happen to people. Well, in *Choose Your Own Nightmare,* you're right in the middle of the action. The scary things are happening to you!

If you had known that little Katie Harper was haunted, you never would have accepted this baby-sitting job. But you've already said yes. It's just you and Katie now.

Don't forget—YOU control your fate. Only you can decide what happens. Follow the instructions at the bottom of each page. The thrills and chills that happen to you will depend on your choices!

Take a deep breath. Are you ready to meet a terrifying toddler? If the answer's yes, then turn to page 1 and . . .
CHOOSE YOUR OWN NIGHTMARE!

You can't believe it! Mrs. Harper from down the street is on the phone, offering you $7.50 an hour to baby-sit her little girl, Katie, for three afternoons a week. She wants you to start at two o'clock tomorrow afternoon.

You could use some extra cash this summer—and $7.50 an hour sounds great!

"I'd love to baby-sit," you tell Mrs. Harper.

Katie is cute. You've seen Mrs. Harper pushing her in her stroller. Mr. Harper is a taxidermist—he stuffs dead animals so that they look real. You think it's pretty weird. But he just opened a shop in the mall, so business must be pretty good. Now that you're going to be baby-sitting at his house, you decide to bike over and have a look.

Turn to page 2.

2

The shop is jammed with fish, birds, and other kinds of animals—all stuffed. You notice a white kitten with black markings on its forepaws. No one would stuff a kitten, you think. But then you see that it is stuffed. Ick! You're staring at it when you hear a sound behind you.

Mr. Harper is standing there, his lips pulled in so that his mouth is just a narrow line on his long, thin face.

"You sure have a lot of, uh, animals here," you say.

"Quite a few." He fixes his eyes on you. "And I've stuffed a lot besides these," he says. "There's only one type of animal I haven't stuffed yet."

"What's that?" you ask.

"A human." He chuckles, but you don't think it's funny.

"I've got to go," you say, and quickly walk out of the shop without even bothering to tell him you'll be baby-sitting for Katie.

Go on to the next page.

Mr. Harper gives you the creeps. After seeing what he's like, you're not sure you want to go into the Harpers' house alone. Maybe you should call your friend Lisa, who lives a couple of doors down from you. Lisa's not afraid of anything. But if you ask her to come along, she'll want to split the money with you.

Ring up Lisa on page 9.

Or go to the Harpers' alone on page 17.

4

You're lying on the ground. You're not dead, but you feel as though you might as well be. Someone's talking to you.

"Are you okay? You're all scratched up. I'll get some antiseptic ointment for you." It's Mrs. Harper. She's standing over you. She must have found you lying there as she was coming up the walk.

You struggle to your feet.

"What are you doing out here anyway?" she asks. "Where's Katie?"

"Oh, Katie's inside the house," you say, hoping you're right.

Mrs. Harper hurries inside as you stumble along behind her.

"Katie!" she calls, "I'm home!" Suddenly she turns on you. "Where *is* Katie?"

If you explain everything that's happened,
turn to page 63.

If you say, "Katie must be up in her room,"
turn to page 5.

"Katie must be up in her room," you lie.

"Are you sure?" Mrs. Harper demands. Her face is filled with anger. Then her expression changes. Her hand flies to her mouth. She lets out a gasp.

"What?" you ask.

Her eyes narrow. An unhappy look comes over her face. "Yes, I'm sure Katie's in her room," she says softly. "Here's your pay—fifteen dollars for two hours." She hands you the money.

You stuff the money in your pocket and watch as Mrs. Harper hurries upstairs. Then you head for home. You're glad to get away from this place, but you're worried about whether you did the right thing. Katie might have run away, or gotten hurt. If Mrs. Harper can't find her, you could be in big trouble!

When you get home you sit by the phone, half expecting her to call.

Considering what happens, maybe it would be better if you didn't turn to page 79.

6

"Congratulations!" the computer voice says. "You've passed the shrinkage test!"

You begin to feel light-headed. You put your hand on the desk to steady yourself.

Katie leans over you, patting your head.

"Poor baby-sitter," she says, stroking your face.

You manage to turn the power off on the computer. The person vanishes. You suddenly feel better—as if your energy level has been given a boost.

"Come on," you say, grabbing Katie's hand. You lead her back to the living room. Katie sits down, giggling.

"Would you like to play with one of your toys?" you ask.

Turn to page 30.

"I'll be right back, Katie," you say. You head for the front hall. Mrs. Harper's note is on the table.

Instructions for Baby-sitters

Katie is a good little girl, but she sometimes has bad dreams, even when she's awake. Don't be frightened if she screams or if she stares at you. This is her way of making friends. Just get her some juice and crackers in the kitchen. You can take her out in the yard or in her stroller.

No television.

Katie can talk very well, and she'll show you what she likes to do.

Mrs. Harper

P.S. Katie may bite or scratch. Be careful.

So that's why I'm getting paid so much, you think.

You walk back into the living room. Katie is gone! A second later you hear a loud crash in the kitchen.

Find out what's wrong on page 76.

8

On your way home, you and Lisa discuss what happened. It's obvious that Katie is a very strange little girl. You can't help worrying about what might be in store for you if you go back there again.

If you return tomorrow, turn to page 37.

If you decide to quit, turn to page 62.

You get on the phone to Lisa and tell her about the baby-sitting job.

"How much is in it for me?" she asks.

"I get seven-fifty an hour. I'll give you half—that's three-seventy-five."

"Four is my minimum," says Lisa.

"That's not fair!" you blurt out. "I'm the one who got the job. Why should you get paid more than me?"

"Take it or leave it," Lisa tells you.

If you feel like it, just say, "No deal, Lisa," and turn to page 17.

OR, keep reading . . .

You hate the idea of Lisa making more than you. But you may need her.

"Oh, all right," you say. "Meet me at the Harpers' tomorrow at two o'clock."

Meet Lisa on page 16.

10

You hurry toward the TV. Katie stares at you with big, glassy eyes.

"Katie—" you start to say. She jumps. You catch her in your arms, but she's amazingly heavy. The two of you crash to the floor.

"Oww!" you cry as your head hits the sharp corner of a wooden block. You gently touch your scalp. At least you're not bleeding. Then you look up at Katie. She's giggling and laughing as if you were the funniest thing in the world.

"Well, at least one of us is having fun," you say, looking at your watch. You hope Mrs. Harper comes home soon. "Would you like to read a book?" you ask, pointing to a nearby bookshelf.

Katie runs over and returns with a picture book titled *The Happy Little Frog.* She hands the book to you and sits down beside you on the rug.

Turn to page 35.

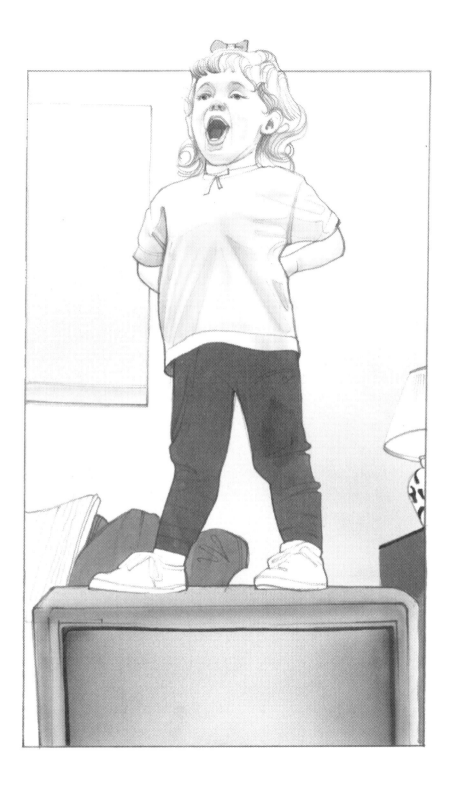

12

Katie leads you upstairs to her bedroom. There's a white wooden bed with a pink quilt on it, a matching chest of drawers, and a huge framed photograph of a tiger on the wall. A two-story dollhouse sits on the floor near the window. It's a perfect model of the Harpers' house!

The front wall of the dollhouse is cut off so you can see the rooms inside. There are little sofas, tables, and chairs—even pictures on the walls. You can see Katie's room in the dollhouse, furnished just like her real room. In it is a model of the dollhouse itself!

"This is pretty cool," you say. "You must like having a dollhouse to play with." As you say this, your eyes blur for just a moment. You blink, making sure you can still see straight.

"We're playing *in* the dollhouse," Katie says happily.

Turn to page 72.

It's another bedroom. On the bed sits a cluster of stuffed toy animals: a turtle, a bunny, a dog, even a stuffed parrot. You thought your little sister had a lot of stuffed animals, but the Harpers have her beat!

You walk over to pick up the bunny. Maybe it will calm Katie down.

Wait a minute.

These aren't stuffed toy animals. They're stuffed *real* animals!

"Yuck!" you cry, jumping back in disgust. They must belong to Mr. Harper. He's even creepier than you'd thought!

Suddenly you hear a loud growl. It sounds like it's right outside the door. Whatever it is, it's not stuffed!

You're curious to find out what's in the hall. But you want to save your skin, too.

If you go investigate the noise, turn to page 52.

If you shut the door to protect yourself, turn to page 64.

14

The blocks are stacked up in a tower four feet high!

There's no way she could have done that! But there's just the two of you here. She *must* have done it.

You kneel down beside her. "That's a great tower," you say. "How did you do that?"

"Kitty made me," she says. She looks frightened.

"What kitty?" you ask.

"Kitty that died."

Then you remember the stuffed kitten in the taxidermy shop. Could the ghost of that kitten be haunting Katie?

Katie fixes her eyes on you. They are changing, and her face is becoming more pointed. Her ears are pricking up, her nose is darkening. And fur is growing on her face. She's changing into a gigantic kitten!

Turn to page 29.

Maybe if you can just get outside, things will straighten out.

But the front door looks about forty feet high! There's no way you can open it. And there's no way you can climb back up the stairs!

Not that it matters. Katie's kitten is coming straight at you.

It was hunting for a mouse. But you'll do.

The End

16

Lisa is waiting for you on the sidewalk by the Harpers' house. Mrs. Harper answers when you ring the doorbell. She is a tall woman with a long, thin face.

"This is my friend, Lisa," you explain. "She's going to help me."

Mrs. Harper's eyes narrow as she looks the two of you over. "All right. Follow me." She leads you into a bright, cheery living room and points to a sweet-looking little girl nestled on some pillows on the sofa. "This is Katie," she says.

Lisa goes over to her. "Oooh, she's so cute!" she says, tickling Katie under the chin.

"There's juice and crackers for Katie in the kitchen," Mrs. Harper says. She looks at her watch. "Oh, I'm late!" She gives a little wave, and suddenly she's out the door.

Turn to page 23.

You pull your bike up to the big, cream-colored house at 39 Bleak Street and rest it against the porch railing.

Mrs. Harper opens the door. She's a tall woman. She leans against the doorway, looking you over.

"Come inside," she finally says.

You follow her into a cheery living room with a bright blue sofa and chairs and a thick rose carpet. A little blond girl is sitting in a miniature rocking chair, rocking and humming. There's a big pile of wooden blocks in front of her. She smiles at you.

"This is Katie," Mrs. Harper says proudly.

Katie tilts her head coyly and waves. She's really cute.

"Stay there, angel," Mrs. Harper says to Katie as she leads you into the kitchen. Beautiful crystal glasses are lined up on the counter. You remind yourself not to let Katie near them.

Turn to page 28.

Katie is on TV! She's standing in the middle of a rain forest! The camera zooms in. Her chubby face fills the screen.

This must be just a videotape. But how did it get in the VCR? Katie couldn't have put it in, could she?

You move closer to the screen, staring at the TV Katie. She comes closer, too, staring at you. Closer. Closer. She steps right out of the screen!

"No!" you cry. You reel backward, stumbling as you lose your balance. She's there, right in front of you, her eyes like searchlights beaming into your brain.

"Get away from me!" you scream.

"What is *wrong* with you?" a voice demands. You spin around and see Mrs. Harper, her face filled with rage. You look back at Katie, who is standing in front of the TV set. Tears are running down her chubby little face.

"Why were you screaming like that?" Mrs. Harper shouts. She points toward the door. "Go home, and never come here again!"

Turn to page 46.

You run upstairs and stop in front of the nearest door. You open it a crack and look inside. It must be Katie's bedroom. A teddy bear is propped on a small, white wooden bed. There's a big dollhouse next to one of the windows.

You glance at the half-open closet door, then bend over to look under the bed. Something runs out of the closet. It's the kitten you saw earlier, mewing softly. You try to pick it up, but your hand passes right through it, as if it wasn't there!

It's not a kitten. It's a kitten's ghost!

Run downstairs to page 39.

By the time you get upstairs, the squealing has stopped. Across from you is a closed door. A little plaque on it reads KATIE'S PLACE.

You open the door a crack. There's no sign of Katie. You see a white wooden bed with a frilly pink quilt on it, a little desk and matching chest of drawers, and a big dollhouse near the window. You check under the bed. She's not there.

Looking up, you find yourself staring at a huge photograph of a tiger on the wall. It looks incredibly real, rearing up as if it's about to pounce, teeth bared. Its claws seem to reach out from the picture. *How could anyone sleep in a room with that?*

Suddenly the tiger snarls!

Wait a minute. You must be imagining things. But that idea scares you almost as much as the tiger!

You quickly back out of the room. The squealing has started again. It's coming from the room across the hall. Slowly you open the door.

Turn to page 13.

22

You leap for the cedar tree. Sharp twigs scratch your face, but you manage to grab a branch and swing in toward the trunk. At that moment you see Katie running back toward the house.

Then you lose your grip.

You're falling, grasping helplessly at branches along the way.

CRASH!

Turn to page 4 to see if this is the end.

"This is the cutest kid I've ever seen," says Lisa. She sits down on the couch and scoops up Katie.

You nod. "Yeah, she is pretty adorable."

"You—are—so—cute," Lisa chants, bouncing Katie up and down on her knee. Katie gurgles happily.

You walk over to turn on the TV—and hear a bloodcurdling scream.

It's Lisa!

Find out why on page 55.

24

"All right. How do we get in?" you ask. Your vision blurs for a moment. You blink.

"We already in it," says Katie.

"You're not making sense," you tell her. You sit down on Katie's bed. "I'm getting dizzy," you add, holding your head in your hands.

"Let's play in the dollhouse," she says, pointing at it.

"No! *I can't take it anymore!*" you scream.

"What's wrong with you?" a grown-up voice demands. You look up—it's Mrs. Harper.

Think about what you will tell her while you turn to page 60.

You stop in your tracks and try to calm yourself. You've got to get outside—not only outside the dollhouse, but outside the Harpers' house. Then maybe everything will get back to normal.

"Katie," you say, trying to keep your voice steady. "Let's go out and play in the yard."

She shakes her head. "Dollhouse doesn't have a yard."

"I don't care!" you say. "We're going outside if I have to carry you!"

"*WHHHHHAAAA!*" she wails, jumping up and down and shaking her chubby fists.

You don't feel like a baby-sitter anymore. You feel like a prisoner! You're tempted to forget about Katie and just try to get outside. Back to the real world.

If you run out of the room and try to get outdoors, turn to page 53.

If you stay with Katie in the dollhouse, turn to page 50.

"Thanks, Mrs. Harper." You stuff the money in your pocket. "I hope Katie will be all right." You turn, leave the house, and start biking toward home, wondering what's going on with this family! Is Mrs. Harper crazy? Or is she right?

As you pedal home, you get the feeling someone's watching you. It gives you the creeps. And when you walk in the front door of your house, you have the strange sensation that someone is walking beside you.

You jog upstairs and open your door.

Turn to page 49.

You take Katie's hand and lead her out to the kitchen. You can still hear the puppy squealing upstairs.

At least you think that's what it is.

"Katie, what's making that noise?" you ask as you take out a carton of orange juice from the fridge. "Katie?"

She doesn't answer. You turn around. She's gone!

"Katie!" you yell, dropping the carton and running back to the living room.

No sign of her.

"Where are you hiding?" you call.

You hear a noise on the stairs. You race into the hall and look up the staircase.

She's not there.

You run up the stairs.

Turn to page 20.

"There's juice and applesauce for Katie in the fridge," Mrs. Harper tells you. She grabs her car keys from a hook. "I've left instructions on the hall table, but there's one other thing I think you should know."

She pauses a moment. "A few months ago, Katie's kitten died. It was very hard on her, and sometimes she thinks the kitten is still alive." Mrs. Harper sighs.

"That's too bad," you murmur.

Mrs. Harper glances at her watch. "Oh, I've got to run. I'm late." She gives you a smile. "Remember, the instructions are on the table. You'll do fine." She hurries out of the room. The front door slams behind her.

A second later you hear Katie scream.

Turn to page 59.

You rub your eyes. When you look again, Katie looks normal.

What a relief!

A few moments later, Mrs. Harper returns. You don't mention your weird experience. She pays you, and in another minute you're on your way.

On the way home you touch your face. It feels soft . . . and hairy! In fact, you'd swear fur is growing on it. This can't be!

A few seconds later you bike up your driveway. Fortunately no one's home. You rush to the bathroom and look in the mirror.

A giant kitten stares back at you! Is this real, or are you going crazy?

Which would be better? you wonder.

Going crazy? Turn to page 43.

Being a cat? Turn to page 66.

30

"I have a dollhouse," Katie says.

"Want to show it to me?"

She nods. "You can come in it."

"It must be a big dollhouse," you say.

Katie stares at you. "It not big," she says firmly.

You're curious about this dollhouse, but Katie's stare gives you a creepy feeling. She looks almost . . . evil.

What now?

Ask Katie to show you her dollhouse?
Turn to page 12.

Go out to play in the yard? Turn to page 34.

Take her for a ride in her stroller? Turn to page 85.

You race over to the Harpers' on your bike, pumping as hard as you can. In a few minutes the house comes into view.

But it doesn't look quite right. The grass has grown about a foot since you left, and the paint has faded and chipped. It's a real mess. A FOR SALE sign is stuck in the lawn. You rattle the front doorknob and peer in a broken window-pane. All the furniture is gone!

Behind you a car honks. You turn around. The driver yells something.

Find out what on page 84.

"I wouldn't feel right getting paid until I make sure Katie is all right," you tell Mrs. Harper. You go to the foot of the stairs. "Katie!" you call.

No answer. Now you're more worried than ever.

"You can go home. I know she's fine," Mrs. Harper says sharply. She tugs at your sleeve. She's behaving very suspiciously—as if there's something about Katie she doesn't want you to know. But you're determined to find the little girl.

You race up the stairs, thinking she may have gone to her room. Mrs. Harper is right behind you. You're about halfway up when she grabs your T-shirt and pulls you back down. "I *said* you could go home," she shrieks.

You twist your body, trying to get free. Mrs. Harper clutches the banister to keep from falling. You break away and race to the top step.

Turn to page 75.

"Let's play in the yard," you tell Katie.

The backyard is quite nice. There's a jungle gym with swings and a slide, and a curving tunnel shaped like a caterpillar. You can crawl into the caterpillar's head and come out its tail.

"Go in the caterpillar," Katie says.

"You first," you say.

"No, *you* first—I scared."

"If you're scared, let's not go in at all," you say.

"You go," she answers.

"All right," you say reluctantly. You squat down and crawl into the tunnel. It's barely big enough for you to move through. Soon it's completely dark inside.

You keep crawling along. You'll be out the other end in a few seconds. But the tunnel is longer than you expected. You'd turn around, but there's no room.

On and on you crawl. You definitely should have reached the end by now. You wiggle a little farther. "Are you close behind me?" you call back to Katie.

No answer.

Crawl on to page 57.

You start reading out loud.

"Once there was a happy little frog. One day it was sitting on a lily pad when a crocodile came along. The crocodile opened its great mouth and snapped its great jaws and chopped the happy little frog to bits."

Katie starts laughing. You give her a strange look. "It's not funny," you say.

"I want juice!" she blurts out.

Before you can answer, you hear a loud squealing upstairs. It sounds like a puppy whose paw has just been stepped on.

"Is that your puppy?" you ask Katie. "We'd better go see."

She scowls at you, shaking her chubby little fists. "I want juice! I want juice! I want juice!"

The squealing from upstairs gets louder.

If you get Katie some juice, turn to page 27.

If you investigate the noise upstairs, turn to page 19.

36

Blue sky! You climb out and look around in amazement. You don't know how, but the tunnel has opened up in your own backyard! You can't believe it. But it must be true. You hear your mother's voice.

"I told you not to go down in that old well!"

You shrug your shoulders. You don't know what to say.

Your mom walks over to you. "Besides, aren't you supposed to be baby-sitting at the Harpers'?"

You're so amazed to find yourself back home you've almost forgotten that you left Katie alone! You've got to go back and see if she's okay!

Turn to page 77.

When you arrive the next afternoon, you find Lisa there ahead of you. Mrs. Harper has already left.

You walk into the living room. Katie is playing happily with her blocks on the rug. Lisa is on the sofa watching.

You plop down next to Katie. "Want to build a house?" you ask. You start piling blocks.

"Hey, look!" Lisa cries. She points at the ceiling. You see a large wet spot that gets larger as you look at it. Only then do you hear the sound of running water upstairs.

"Stay still," you tell Katie. You and Lisa race upstairs and run to the bathroom off the hallway. The shower is on full force. Water is spilling over the edge of the tub and spreading across the floor.

"Turn it off!" Lisa screams. You reach for the faucet, but before you can touch it, it stops by itself. Lisa gasps.

"How could—?"

You're cut off by a scream from downstairs.

Turn to page 67.

38

You run as fast as you can. But the stroller rolls even faster.

Your sneakers pound the pavement as you fly down the road.

"Katie!" you cry. You begin to catch up. Soon you're only a few feet away.

Just as you're about to grab the stroller, it jumps the curb and tips over. The strap gives way, and Katie sprawls out onto the street! You hear a tremendous horn blast. A gigantic truck is coming right at her!

You race to pull Katie away. As you reach for her, she breaks free and leaps back onto the sidewalk.

The truck hits you.

SMUSH!

As you take your last breath, you see Katie standing on the sidewalk, smiling happily down at you.

"Bye-bye," she says.

The End

"Help!" you scream as you run at breakneck speed down the stairs. Katie is standing in the hallway. She smiles up at you.

"You loud," she says calmly.

You look back but see nothing. "I—I thought there was a kitten up there," you say, gasping for air. Your neck is dripping with sweat.

Katie nods. "Here kitty, kitty, kitty," she calls.

You look up the stairs. There it is again—the ghost kitten. You watch in amazement as it floats down the steps. You reach down to feel it, but suddenly it disappears.

Katie grins at you.

"Where did the kitten go?" you ask her.

"Bye, kitty. Bye-bye," she says.

The front door opens.

Turn to page 48.

40

You clutch your blanket to your chest. You swallow hard. You try to calm yourself, hoping you are just imagining things. Then, softly, you call her name.

"Katie? Katie? Are you there?"

"I'm here," she answers. "I always be here."

The End

It's hopeless. You lie down and start to cry.

After a while you realize that crying isn't going to help you any. In fact, it could get you into even more trouble.

And it does. Suddenly you hear a man's voice in the room. The voice is actually more like a cruel laugh.

You look up. It's Mr. Harper, home from his taxidermy shop. He doesn't speak. But there's a wild look in his eyes. His mouth is twisted into a cruel smile.

"There you are," he finally says. "All ready to be stuffed."

The End

If you've gone crazy, you need help. And the only person who might understand is Lisa. Frantically, you dial her number.

"Lisa, come over fast. I think I've turned into a giant kitten!"

"This I've got to see," she says. "Hang on, I'll be there in a minute."

You force yourself to look in the mirror again. You still have a furry head, pointed ears, and whiskers!

Lisa is knocking at the door. You run to open it.

"Well?" you ask. Lisa will probably faint.

"You don't look like a kitten!" she says, laughing.

"Really?" you ask, touching your cheeks. "I must be going crazy!"

"Tell me what happened today at the Harpers'," she says.

You describe everything, especially how Katie seemed to turn into a kitten.

Lisa listens carefully. "Maybe the ghost of the kitten was haunting Katie, and now it's haunting you."

After thinking about this, turn to page 82.

44

You go back to your room, lie on your bed, and close your eyes. Then you think hard—*wake up, wake up, wake up!*

"Wake up," says your mom. "You've been napping long enough."

It worked—you're out of the nightmare!

"Besides," your mom goes on, "Mrs. Harper is on the phone. She has a baby-sitting job for you. She'll pay seven-fifty an hour! What should I tell her?"

If you say, "Tell her yes," turn to page 17.

Otherwise, just say, "NO THANKS!" and this is

The End

There are little eyes for little animals and big eyes for big animals. Looking at them makes you feel slightly sick. You scoop them up and put them back in the bucket. This makes Katie angry. She starts to wail again.

Lisa races back in. "What did you do to her?" she asks.

"Nothing!" you answer. At that moment Katie pounces on something on the rug next to the sofa. It's a mouse! Katie clutches it, then drops it. The mouse scoots under the sofa.

She turns, scowling, while you and Lisa stand there gaping at what you've just seen.

A moment later the front door opens, and Mrs. Harper walks in. Katie has started playing with her blocks. Her mother picks her up and hugs her, then turns to you and Lisa. "You two have been such good baby-sitters, I'm giving you each a dollar bonus. See you tomorrow."

"Sure," you say.

Turn to page 8.

It takes you about half a second to race outside. The door slams shut behind you.

Biking toward home, you see your friend Lisa walking down the street.

She waves. "Hey, I called you—your mom said you were baby-sitting for the Harpers."

You bike up alongside her. Suddenly she turns pale.

"What are you doing?" she cries. "Why are you staring at me like that?"

You don't mean to, but you snarl, sounding like an angry cat. "Lisa—" you start to explain, but she lets out a shriek and runs off.

You hurry on home, drop your bike near the front door, and run to the bathroom. You stand for a long time looking at yourself in the mirror. No wonder Lisa was frightened! Your eyes are big, fixed, and glassy, and you know the reason why. Whatever was haunting Katie is now haunting you.

The End

You rush to the other window. It looks out on another wall, and on it is a huge photograph of a tiger. Through every window you see what you'd see if you were in Katie's room *in* the dollhouse!

Now you're *sure* she has evil powers.

You run to the door. The hallway looks the way it did before, but that could be because you're in the dollhouse. You'll have to go downstairs and go out the front door to make sure. You tear out of the room.

"Where you going?" Katie cries. "You said you play with me in dollhouse!"

Turn to page 25.

48

Mrs. Harper comes in. Katie bounces up and down in front of her. "Mommy! Mommy! Kitty not in me anymore!"

Mrs. Harper breaks into a broad smile. "That's wonderful, darling." She pats Katie's head and gives her a hug. Then she reaches in her purse and hands you a twenty-dollar bill. "You've done more than I dreamed possible," she says. "I'm so happy you've taken over the kitten."

Huh? What is she talking about?

"Taken over the kitten?" you exclaim. "But where is it?"

She draws the palm of her hand gently across your face. "It's yours now," she says sweetly. "It's *in* you."

The End

You spend the rest of the day in your room playing video games. When you finally fall asleep that night, you dream that a giant kitten is stalking you. You thrash about, desperate to escape its pointy claws. You're about to be torn to shreds when you wake up.

"Just a nightmare," you mumble groggily. You fumble for the light on the nightstand. *Click.* You rub your eyes and look around. Everything's fine. You turn off the light and try to get back to sleep. You're just about to doze off when you hear a tiny voice.

"I'm here."

Katie!

Turn to page 73.

"All right," you tell Katie. "We'll stay here. What do you want to do?"

"Play in the dollhouse," Katie says in a sweet voice.

"I thought that's what we were doing," you say wearily.

"*This* dollhouse," she says brightly, pointing to the model dollhouse—what you thought was the dollhouse inside the dollhouse!

This is starting to give you a headache.

If you go along with her, turn to page 24.

If you don't, turn to page 56.

You stay with Katie. She grabs your hand and starts leading you through the house. You're amazed at how strong her grip is.

You follow her along the carpeted hallway into a small room. There's a bookshelf filled with books, a coffee table, and a small plaid couch. Against the wall sits a desk with a computer. Katie heads straight for it.

"On," she says, flipping on the power switch.

"I don't think we're supposed to touch this, Katie," you say, reaching over to turn the computer off.

"On!" says Katie, brushing your hand away.

The computer screen lights up.

"Blink and shrink!" the computer voice says.

A cartoon person appears on the screen. Katie clicks on the person's eyeball. The person gets smaller and smaller.

Katie giggles. "Fun!" she says.

Click onto page 6.

Cautiously you step out into the hallway, then jump back in surprise. There's no big animal. Just Katie, smiling up at you.

"What you do in that room?" she scolds. "I'm going to tell Mommy!"

"Go ahead," you say, annoyed. "I was just looking for you!"

"That room for my pets!" she shrieks. "You bad!"

Tiny as she is, she starts pushing you. She has some power you can't understand. You have a feeling that if you don't obey her, something terrible will happen.

Turn to page 70.

"I'll be right back," you tell her. You run out of the room, down the stairs, and whip open the front door.

And scream in terror.

You're in Katie's room again. Except you're only three inches tall! The bed, the chest of drawers—even Katie's toys—all loom above you.

You've been shrunk to the scale of the dollhouse. You're not even as tall as its front door!

How could this have happened? Then it hits you. Blink and Shrink. That weird computer game shrunk you!

You run down the hall of the real house. It's a long way because you're so tiny. You look down the staircase in fear. Each step is twice as high as you are! You jump anyway, step by step. Sixteen hops brings you to the bottom. You race toward the front door.

Quick! Turn to page 15.

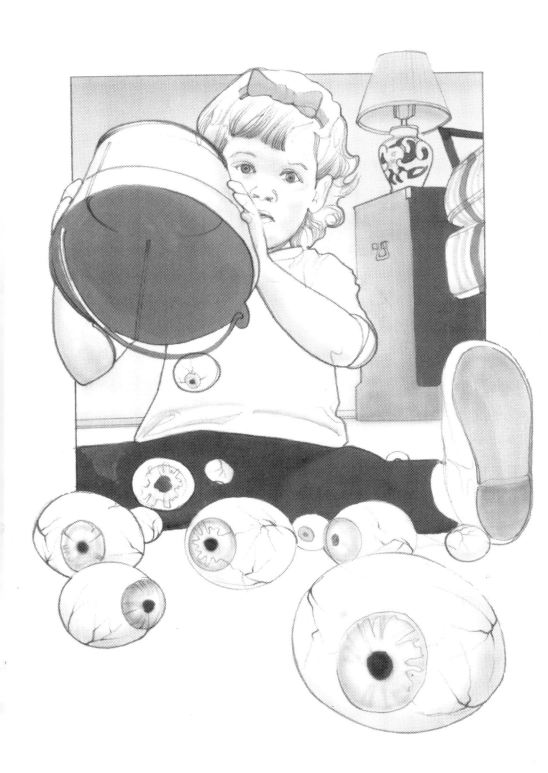

"She bit me!" Lisa throws Katie on the couch and jumps away. Katie lets out a wail so loud it hurts your ears. You run to pick her up.

"No biting, Katie," you say. "That's bad." You turn to Lisa. "You can't just throw her like that!"

"Well, I need a Band-Aid," Lisa huffs. She hurries toward the kitchen. You try to distract Katie's attention, hoping you won't get bitten, too.

There are some toys on the lower shelf of the bookcase. You carry Katie over there and set her down. "Want to play with one of these?"

Katie reaches in and pulls out a small plastic bucket. It's full of glass eyes. Mr. Harper probably uses them when he stuffs animals. Katie dumps them on the rug and starts to sift through them.

Turn to page 45.

"No! No more shrinking! We're going out-side!" You pick up Katie. She's heavier than you'd have thought, but you manage to carry her, kicking and screaming, down the stairs, through the hall, and outdoors—the *real* out-doors!

You and Katie are your regular size again! You wouldn't give in to her, and that must have broken her hold on you!

Your troubles aren't over, though. Here comes Mrs. Harper. Katie is screaming her lungs out.

"I saw you dragging my child around!" she says indignantly. She picks up Katie and strokes her hair. "How is my little angel?" she asks, and gives you a ferocious look. "I'll never use you to baby-sit Katie again!"

You wonder if you should try to explain everything that's happened but decide it's not worth the effort. You head for home, glad to be out of the dollhouse, and the Harpers' house, for good.

And that's the last you see of her.

Except in your nightmares.

The End

You crawl on anyway. You have no other choice. And then . . .

Light! The tunnel slopes upward. The plastic walls give way to large stones, wedged together. Soon the tunnel is heading almost straight up. The stones stick out a little so you can plant your feet and get handholds.

You begin to climb.

Keep climbing to page 36.

A second later you're laughing with them. And there's no way to stop yourself. You and Lisa have become haunted baby-sitters.

The End

You hurry to the living room, almost tripping over something on your way. You look around in time to see a little white kitten scoot behind the sofa. It's funny that Mrs. Harper didn't mention that Katie got a new kitten, you think.

Katie is standing on the seat of her rocker, but nothing seems to be wrong.

"Did the kitten frighten you?" you ask, picking her up.

"Kitten here," she murmurs. "You bad?"

You chuckle. "I'm not bad, and you're not bad. We're both good!"

Katie giggles.

"Do you want to play with the blocks?" you ask.

"Meow," she purrs, sounding just like a kitten. It amazes you how she imitates it so exactly.

At that moment you remember that you haven't read the instructions yet.

Read Mrs. Harper's instructions on page 7.

Skip them for now and turn to page 51.

60

"Um, we were just pretending," you say nervously.

Mrs. Harper looks at Katie. "Did you have a good time, darling?" she asks.

"Yes, Mommy." Katie smiles sweetly.

"Good," says Mrs. Harper. She takes fifteen dollars from her purse and hands it to you. "Thanks for doing such a good job. We'll see you tomorrow then. Same time all right?"

"Sure," you say. You're feeling a bit better—maybe you're *not* in the dollhouse.

"Bye," says Katie.

"Bye," you say. You hurry downstairs, open the front door—and step out of the dollhouse into Katie's bedroom.

A giant-sized Katie is sitting on the bed. She's smiling at you, but you don't smile back. Gently, she picks you up and puts you back in her dollhouse.

The End

62

When you get home you call Mrs. Harper and tell her you've decided to quit. "You can't!" she pleads. "Lisa already canceled and I have to go to the doctor. It could be a matter of life or death!"

"All right, if it's so important," you say. "I'll work one more day."

You show up as promised. You feel better after a half hour of watching Katie play happily with her blocks. Everything's going fine. You try to show Katie how to stack her blocks up high, but she keeps knocking them over, giggling so hard you're afraid she'll get the hiccups.

"Juice," she says.

"Stay right here, I'll get it." You go to the kitchen and pour some juice for her. When you get back you can't believe what you see!

Turn to page 14.

You explain everything that's happened, hoping to convince Mrs. Harper that you've *tried* to be a good baby-sitter.

You're not convincing her. Her face reddens, her eyes bulge. The veins on her neck look like they're going to pop.

Meanwhile, her arm goes up. She's holding a handbag with heavy leather straps. She starts to swing it. You back up fast. Then she bursts into tears!

"It's my fault," she cries. "I'm sorry. It's—it's just so hard living with Katie, and hiding the fact that . . ." She stops and reaches into her handbag.

You step back farther. What is she reaching for?

She pulls out a tissue and blows her nose.

"What fact, Mrs. Harper?" you whisper.

Turn to page 74.

You lock the door and glance around, half expecting the stuffed animals to come alive. They don't. But now, outside the door, you hear a loud scraping, like a big cat raking its claws against the wood.

Either you've gone crazy, or this house has turned into a zoo!

You rush to the window, wondering whether you can get out that way. There's a big cedar tree growing close by. You could jump and land in it—you'd get scratched, but you could probably get down without breaking a leg.

And you're going to have to get down! You've just spotted Katie on the front walk, heading toward the street!

Turn to page 80.

You open the door and race downstairs. You're halfway down when you hear a noise— lots of noises—coming from below. Animals growling, birds squawking, insects buzzing— even running water! As if you'd been dropped into a rain forest!

You take the steps two at a time. Your heart is racing. You swipe the sweat from your brow.

The noise is coming from the TV! You wonder who turned it on, but you can't think about that. You've got to get Katie before she walks out into the street.

But you can't.

Something is holding your eyes to the screen!

Turn to page 18.

66

You decide you'd rather be a kitten than crazy.

You get your wish. You're four inches tall; you have four legs, a tail, a little black nose, sharp teeth, claws, and whiskers; and you like catnip.

A little girl is holding you, stroking your back. It's Katie!

She's so sweet. She's going to be fun to haunt.

The End

When you get downstairs, you find that Katie isn't screaming. She's laughing! The screaming was coming from the TV. A monster with long, scaly arms is strangling people on a street.

"No TV!" you say, and reach for the remote. Katie howls.

You push the off button. But it doesn't work. Instead you see another movie. Waves of slime are breaking on a beach. People are running from it, screaming as the waves wash over them, drowning them in dark blue goo.

"Nice!" says Katie. She gurgles happily.

You push hard on the off button, only to get back to the first movie. Now the monster is crushing people under its elephant-sized feet.

"This is crazy!" you shout. You wedge between the wall and the TV set, planning to pull the plug. But it's already unplugged!

"Lisa, help me!" you cry. But Lisa is sitting on the floor next to Katie, laughing with her at the horror on the screen.

Turn to page 58.

You leap back in pain. "Ouch! That hurt!" you yell. Without thinking, you let go of the stroller to rub your hand. In a flash, the stroller, with Katie in it, is rolling down the hill. For a split second you don't care. Then you realize you *have* to care.

"Wait!" you scream, running after it. But it's gathering speed!

Turn to page 38.

70

She pushes you toward the open door of a large closet. Suddenly, with strength you wouldn't think possible, she shoves you in.

SLAM! CLICK!

Darkness.

You grope around for the light. You can't feel a light switch. You can't even feel the door!

What can you do? Find out on page 83.

If this is a nightmare, it's the most realistic one you've ever had!

"I—I'm sorry Katie—I—I thought you must be all right," you stammer.

Her dark eyes flash with anger. "I only two years old! I go to window, wanna find my mommy. And I fell. Fell. Fell! DEAD!"

You shrink back. This has to be a nightmare—you've got to wake up! You leap out of bed and turn on the light.

She's still there!

"I dead," Katie says. "Kitty haunted me. Now I going to haunt *you*!"

The End

"You mean we're *pretending* we're in it," you say gently.

Katie shakes her head. "We not pretending! We in my room in the dollhouse. Look out the window."

You go along with her game and look out the window as she asks.

And gasp.

No trees.

No grass.

No sky.

Instead you're staring out at a high wall and a pink carpeted floor with an enormous bed covered in a huge pink quilt!

Turn to page 47.

You reach for the light so fast you knock it over. The bulb gives off a brilliant flash and burns out. In that instant you see Katie standing beside your bed, a happy smile on her face. Then everything goes black.

A chill of fear grips your body.

Hurry to page 40.

74

She sniffles a little. To your surprise, she hands you a twenty-dollar bill. "Never mind. You've done the best you can," she murmurs.

You hesitate, feeling guilty. You feel it's not quite right to take the money while Katie is still missing.

"Please, Mrs. Harper—what were you going to tell me?" you persist.

Turn to page 78.
Turn to page 78.

"Katie! Katie! Where are you?" you shout.

You throw open the door to Katie's room.

She is sitting on the floor, surrounded by tiny dead mice. One of them is still alive, struggling to get free. Katie is pinning it to the rug with her fingers!

She looks up at you and giggles. You don't know whether to stay or run. Then you feel Mrs. Harper's hand on your shoulder.

"Now you know," she says in a low voice. "And you must never, ever tell."

"Tell . . . ?"

The struggling mouse has gone limp. To your horror, Katie begins to gnaw on it!

Mrs. Harper does nothing to stop her. "The kitten makes her act this way," she says in a low voice. "The kitten she killed."

The End

You already know what's wrong. Katie must have knocked over those crystal glasses! You run to the kitchen.

There's no sign of Katie. The glasses are still on the counter.

Then you hear a scream from the living room. *"Ahhh!"*

You rush toward the sound. Katie is nowhere to be seen.

You look behind the sofa. Behind all the chairs. Behind the curtains. Nothing. Then you see her—standing on the television set!

How did she get up there?

Turn to page 10.

"Right, Mom." There is no use trying to explain the situation. You hurry to the front of your house—and get another shock. Your bike—the one you rode to the Harpers'—is leaning up against the garage! How did it get back here? Come to think of it, how did you get back here?

What's been happening seems real, but maybe it's all just been some weird nightmare. If so, you'd better try to wake up!

Go to the Harpers' house on page 31.

Or try to wake up on page 44.

78

"Well, you might as well know," she says softly. "Katie is haunted."

You gasp. "You've got to be kidding me."

Mrs. Harper shakes her head.

This sounds ridiculous. But considering the strange things that have been happening, maybe it's not. You'd like to take the twenty dollars and go home, but you have a feeling that if you do, your troubles may not be over.

---

*If you take the money and head for home,
turn to page 26.*

*If you decide you've got to see Katie before you go,
turn to page 33.*

Mrs. Harper doesn't call.

But Katie does.

At midnight, a noise wakes you from a deep sleep. You sit up in bed and rub your eyes. Katie is standing in front of you, lit by the pale moonlight streaming through the bedroom window.

"You left me," she says.

Turn to page 71.

80

You throw open the window. "Katie!" you scream. "Come back here!"

She turns and stares up at you. A dark shadow passes over her face. It makes you shiver.

"You bad!" she shrieks. "I going to tell Mommy!"

Things couldn't be worse!

If you dare to jump for it, leap to page 22.

If you open the door and run downstairs, turn to page 65.

If you lie down on the bed and cry, turn to page 42.

You're still thinking when Lisa starts touching her face. She looks worried.

"What's wrong?" you ask.

"I'm growing whiskers!" she cries. "And fur!"

"I don't see anything," you say.

She pats different parts of her face. "My nose is different. And my ears!"

"Lisa, this can't be."

She brushes past you, looks in the hall mirror, and runs screaming out of the house.

You go to the mirror. *You* look perfectly normal. What a relief! You step outside to find Lisa. She's sitting on the grass crying. Your dog is nuzzling her, making her feel better, you hope. A moment later he runs up to you.

"Hey, boy," you say.

Normally he'd be wagging his tail. But this time, he just meows.

The End

The only thing you can do is cry for help. "Help!"

Then louder. *"Help!"*

Then as loud as you can! *"HELP!"*

You cry out again.

And again.

And again.

There is no end.

"The people who lived there moved out of town!" he shouts as he drives away.

You take another look. Suddenly something furry brushes against your ankle. It's a white kitten with black markings on its front paws. Katie's kitten!

"Meow." It purrs, looking up at you.

They must have left it behind, you think.

You peer in the windows again. All is empty and silent. Your mind whirls, thinking about the strange things that have happened.

The kitten continues to rub against your ankles, purring quietly.

What is it about this kitten? It gives you the shivers.

You hop on your bike, anxious to be away from this place. The kitten runs ahead of you. It turns a corner, looking back over its shoulder.

You pump harder.

The kitten runs faster. And you realize it's not just following—it's leading you home!

The End

Katie fusses at first, but finally she agrees to go riding in her stroller. You push her down the street. She's strangely quiet. Maybe she's fallen asleep.

You stop pushing the stroller and take a peek at Katie. She smiles up at you, sweet as can be.

Then you realize you haven't been paying attention to where you're going. You're at the top of High Street, the steepest street in town. You make sure Katie's strapped in tightly.

"This is some hill, isn't it, Katie?" you ask. Your feet begin to pick up speed as you descend.

"*Eee!*" Katie squeals unexpectedly. A moth has landed on her arm. You lean forward to brush it away. But as your hand gets near her, Katie bites you. Hard!

Turn to page 69.